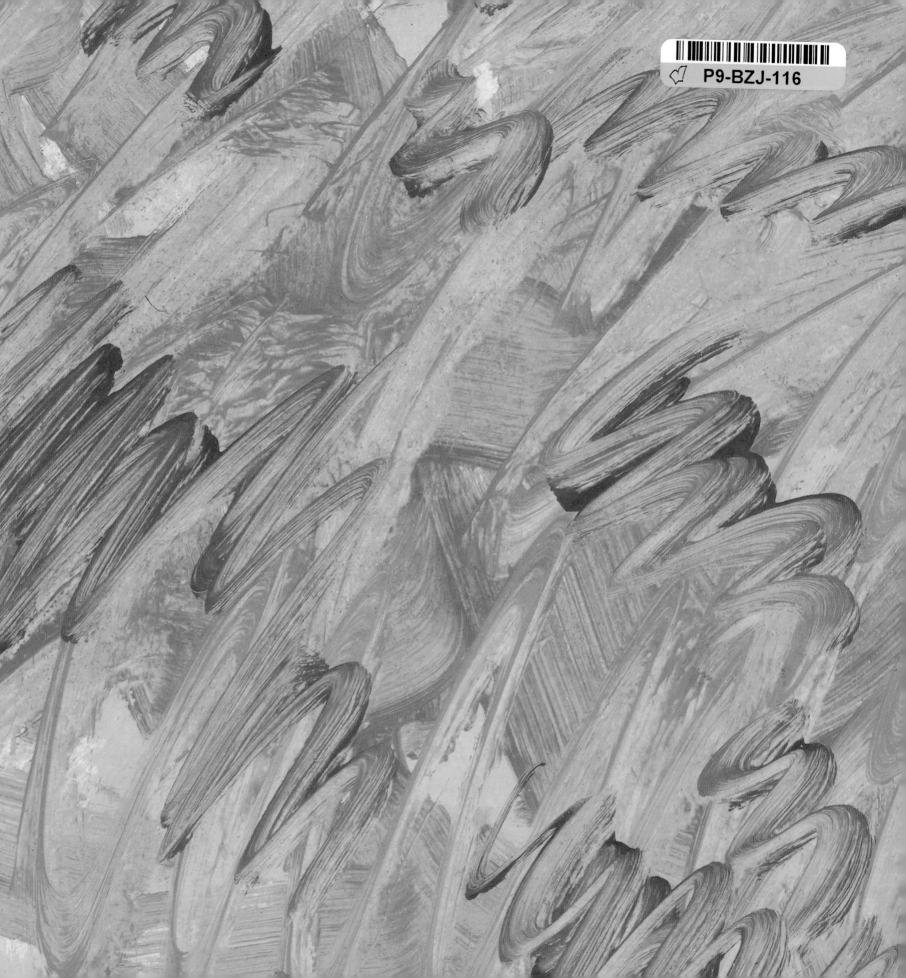

 Aphids are very small insects.
They suck the juice from leaves,
and then the leaves die.
Ladybugs eat aphids.
That's good for trees, shrubs, and
other plants that have leaves.
To the ladybugs I have dedicated this book.
Three cheers for them!

This revised edition has been printed from new separations
made from the original artwork.

Eric Carle's name and his signature logotype are trademarks
of Eric Carle.

For information address HarperCollins Children's Books,
a division of HarperCollins Publishers,
10 East 53rd Street, New York, NY 10022.
www.harpercollinschildrens.com

For more information about Eric Carle and his books and products, please visit: www.eric-carle.com
For information about The Eric Carle Museum of Picture Book Art, please visit: www.carlemuseum.org

This special edition was printed for Kohl's Department Stores, Inc.
(for distribution on behalf of Kohl's Cares, LLC, its wholly owned subsidiary)
by HarperCollins Publishers.

ISBN 978-0-06-204354-2

10 11 12 13 14 SCP 10 9 8 7 6 5 4 3 2 1

CIP information in back of book.

The Grouchy Ladybug

Eric Carle

HarperCollins*Publishers*

It was night and some fireflies danced around the moon.

At five o'clock in the morning the sun came up.
A friendly ladybug flew in from the left. It saw a leaf with many aphids on it,
and decided to have them for breakfast.
But just then a grouchy ladybug flew in from the right.
It too saw the aphids and wanted them for breakfast.

"Good morning," said the friendly ladybug.
"Go away!" shouted the grouchy ladybug. "I want those aphids."
"We can share them," suggested the friendly ladybug.
"No. They're mine, all mine," screamed the grouchy ladybug.
"Or do you want to fight me for them?"

"If you insist," answered the friendly ladybug sweetly.
It looked the other bug straight in the eye.
The grouchy ladybug stepped back.
It looked less sure of itself.
"Oh, you're not big enough for me to fight," it said.
"Then why don't you pick on somebody bigger?"
"I'll do that!" screeched the grouchy ladybug.
"I'll show you!" It puffed itself up and flew off.

At six o'clock
 it met a yellow jacket.
"Hey you," said
 the grouchy ladybug.
"Want to fight?"
"If you insist," said
 the yellow jacket,
 showing its stinger.
"Oh, you're not
 big enough," said
 the grouchy ladybug
 and flew off.

At seven o'clock
it met a stag beetle.
"Hey you," said
the grouchy ladybug.
"Want to fight?"
"If you insist," said
the stag beetle,
opening its jaws.
"Oh, you're not
big enough," said
the grouchy ladybug,
and flew off.

At eight o'clock
it came across
a praying mantis.
"Hey you," said
the grouchy ladybug.
"Want to fight?"
"If you insist," said
the praying mantis,
reaching out with
its long front legs.
"Oh, you're not
big enough," said
the grouchy ladybug
and flew off.

At nine o'clock
it almost flew into
a sparrow.
"Hey you," said
the grouchy ladybug.
"Want to fight?"
"If you insist," said
the sparrow, opening
its sharp beak.
"Oh, you're not
big enough," said
the grouchy ladybug
and flew off.

At ten o'clock
it saw a lobster.
"Hey you," said
the grouchy ladybug.
"Want to fight?"
"If you insist," said
the lobster,
stretching its claws.
"Oh, you're not big enough,"
said the grouchy ladybug
and flew off.

At eleven o'clock
it bumped into a skunk.
"Hey you," said
the grouchy ladybug.
"Want to fight?"
"If you insist," said
the skunk, starting to lift its tail.
"Oh, you're not big enough,"
said the grouchy ladybug
and flew off.

At twelve noon
it spotted a boa constrictor.
"Hey you," said
the grouchy ladybug.
"Want to fight?"
"If you insis-s-s-t," said the snake,
"right after lunch."
"Oh, you're not big enough,"
said the grouchy ladybug
and flew off.

At one o'clock
it happened upon
a hyena.
"Hey you," said
the grouchy ladybug.
"Want to fight?"
"If you insist," said the hyena,
laughing eerily and
showing its teeth.
"Oh, you're not big enough,"
said the grouchy ladybug
and flew off.

At two o'clock
it met a gorilla.
"Hey you," said
the grouchy ladybug.
"Want to fight?"
"If you insist," said the gorilla,
beating its chest.
"Oh, you're not big enough,"
said the grouchy ladybug
and flew off.

At three o'clock
it ran into
a rhinoceros.
"Hey you," said
the grouchy ladybug.
"Want to fight?"
"If you insist," said
the rhinoceros,
lowering its horn.
"Oh, you're not big enough,"
said the grouchy ladybug
and flew off.

At four o'clock
it encountered
an elephant.
"Hey you," said
the grouchy ladybug.
"Want to fight?"
"If you insist," said the elephant,
raising its trunk and
showing its big tusks.
"Oh, you're not big enough,"
said the grouchy ladybug
and flew off.

At five o'clock
it met a whale.
"Hey you," said
the grouchy ladybug.
"Want to fight?"
But the whale
did not answer at all.
"You're not
big enough anyway,"
said the grouchy ladybug
and flew off.

At five fifteen the grouchy ladybug said to one of the whale's flippers, "Hey you, want to fight?"

But it got no answer. So it flew on.

But it got no answer. So it flew on.

At a quarter to six the grouchy ladybug said to the whale's tail, "Hey you, want to fight?"

And the whale's tail gave
the grouchy ladybug
such a SLAP . . .   ss the land.

At six o'clock the grouchy ladybug arrived right back where it had started from.

THANK YOU

"Ah, here you are again," said the friendly ladybug. "You must be hungry. There are still some aphids left. You can have them for dinner."
"Oh, thank you," said the wet, tired, and hungry ladybug.

Soon all the aphids were gone.
"Thank you," said the leaf.
"You are welcome," answered both ladybugs, and they went to sleep.
The fireflies, who had been sleeping all day, came out to dance around the moon.

Library of Congress Cataloging-in-Publication Data

Carle, Eric.
The grouchy ladybug / Eric Carle.
p.   cm.
SUMMARY: A grouchy ladybug,
looking for a fight, challenges everyone
she meets regardless of their size or strength.
ISBN 0-06-027087-X.—ISBN 0-06-443450-8 (pbk.)
ISBN 0-06-027088-8 (lib. bdg.)
[1. Ladybugs—Fiction.   2. Behavior—Fiction.]   I. Title.
PZ7.C21476Gr   1996   95-26581
[E]—dc20   CIP
AC